THE STORY OF DOCTOR DOLITTLE

by HUGH LOFTING

#5 Doctor Dolittle and the Pirates

Adapted by Diane Namm

Illustrated by John Kanzler

STERLING

New York / London
www.sterlingpublishing.com/kids

Library of Congress Cataloging-in-Publication Data Available

Lot #: 10 9 8 7 6 5 4 3 2 1
02/10
Published by Sterling Publishing Co., Inc.
387 Park Avenue South, New York, NY 10016

Distributed in Canada by Sterling Publishing
c/o Canadian Manda Group, 165 Dufferin Street
Toronto, Ontario, Canada M6K 3H6
Distributed in the United Kingdom by GMC Distribution Services
Castle Place, 166 High Street, Lewes, East Sussex, England BN7 1XU
Distributed in Australia by Capricorn Link (Australia) Pty. Ltd.
P.O. Box 704, Windsor, NSW 2756, Australia

Printed in China

Sterling ISBN 978-1-4027-6721-0

For information about custom editions, special sales, premium and corporate purchases, please contact Sterling Special Sales Department at 800-805-5489 or specialsales@sterlingpublishing.com.

Contents

The Leaky Ship

Doctor Dolittle's ship sailed
slowly out to sea.
Doctor Dolittle looked sad.
"What is wrong, Doctor?"
asked the pushmi-pullyu.
"It is hard to leave behind such good
friends," the doctor replied.
He pointed in the direction
of the shore.

"Goodbye!" chattered
Chee-Chee the monkey.
"Safe trip!" squawked Polynesia the parrot.
"Come back soon!" roared Great King Lion.
Circus Crocodile cried and waved.

"You still have us,"
oinked Gub-Gub the pig.
"You're not alone,"
quacked Dab-Dab the duck.

“We’re never alone,” said the
pushmi-pullyu.
Jip the dog barked suddenly.
“Look, a ship!”

Everyone turned.

"Pirates!" exclaimed the doctor.

"All hands on deck!

We must sail away at once!"

The animals tried their hardest
to make the ship go fast.
The sail was up. The wind blew.
But the ship just would not go.

"Water!" barked Jip.

"Oh, dear," said Doctor Dolittle.

"The boat has sprung a leak!

That's why we are moving so slowly."

“What do we do?” oinked Gub-Gub.

“Grab a bucket!” Doctor Dolittle said.

Just then …

… a flock of swallows flew by.
They used their beaks to
pull the ship into a secret bay
that was safe from the pirates.
"How can we thank you?"
the doctor asked.

"Birdseed?" the hungry swallows asked.
"I'm sorry, I don't have any,"
the doctor said.
"But I promise, someday
I will repay you."

Pirates Aboard!

"After all this adventure, I need a nap!"
Doctor Dolittle said, when they
were on the shore.
Gub-Gub and Jip curled up to rest.
So did Doctor Dolittle.
The pushmi-pullyu fell fast asleep.
Dab-Dab went for a salty swim.
Everyone forgot about the pirates.

But the pirates did not forget
about Doctor Dolittle.
They circled the island,
spied the ship, and got on board!

"Ho, ho, ho,"
chuckled the pirate captain.
His name was Barbary Dragon.
He was the most terrible pirate
on the high seas.

"This ship is ours," he declared.
"Take what you like, mates!"
Dab-Dab swam by
and saw the pirates.
"I must tell the doctor," he quacked.

Dab-Dab swam as fast as his
little webbed feet would paddle.
"Doctor Dolittle! Doctor Dolittle,"
he quacked as loudly as he could.

Pirates and Dragons and Sharks, Oh, My!

"Pirates! Pirates on board our ship!"
Dab-Dab quacked
into the doctor's ear.
"Oh, no! What will we do?"

"Don't worry," the doctor
said with a smile.
"Let the pirates have our ship.
I have the perfect plan!"

One by one, the animals
waded into the water
after Doctor Dolittle.
Then they climbed up
the side ladder of the pirate ship
and tiptoed onto the deck!

"Hoist the sail!"
shouted Doctor Dolittle.
The animals ran about.
Quick as a wink, the ship set sail.
The good doctor and the
animals were on their way.
They had a brand new ship!

"Captain, look! They have
our ship!" a pirate said.
"After them!" Barbary Dragon
shouted to the pirates.

"They're getting closer, doctor,"
the animals cried.
"We can't outrun them,"
Doctor Dolittle said.
"What shall we do?"
the animals asked.

"Keep sailing," Doctor Dolittle
told his crew.
"With any luck, they'll sink
before they ever reach us!"
"Stop!" roared the pirate captain.
"Give us back our ship!"

Just then a fin popped up
out of the water.
Then two. Then three.
"Sharks!" a happy Doctor Dolittle said.

The Dragon's Promise

"Doctor Dolittle, can I help you?"
the head shark asked.
"Help me teach this
pirate captain a lesson,"
the good doctor said.
"Certainly," the shark replied.
Soon the sharks had the
leaky ship surrounded.

"I give up!" shouted
the pirate captain.

"Promise me something,"
Doctor Dolittle said.
"No!" the pirate captain said.
The head shark squeezed
the pirate hard.
"Ow. Ow. Okay," the pirate captain agreed.

Doctor Dolittle remembered
the hungry swallows that
had nothing to eat.
"Birdseed farming," the doctor said.
"What? asked the pirate captain.

From that day on, the
pirate captain and his crew
were birdseed farmers.
And the swallows on the
island never went hungry again.
Doctor Dolittle and his crew
sailed off on the pirate ship
in search of Puddleby,
their beloved home.